Tooth Fairy

Peppa and George are eating
their favourite food — spaghetti!

"Slurp! Sloooop!"
"Slurp! Sloooop!"

Suddenly something falls on to
Peppa's plate.

"What's that?" cries Peppa.
"It's your tooth!" Daddy Pig laughs.

"If you put the tooth under your pillow tonight the Tooth Fairy will pay you a visit," says Mummy Pig.

"She will take the tooth and leave you a shiny coin!"

Peppa puts her tooth under
the pillow for the Tooth Fairy.

"Let's stay awake all night and
see the Tooth Fairy," says Peppa.
"Snort!" George giggles.

"George, where's the Tooth Fairy?"
Peppa asks. "She's very late!"

But George is so tired he has fallen
fast asleep.

"I'm not going to go to sleep . . .
I'm . . . zzz zzz," snores Peppa.

When everything is quiet, something appears at the window.

The Tooth Fairy has arrived, but Peppa
is fast asleep.

The Tooth Fairy pushes a shiny coin under the pillow and takes Peppa's tiny tooth.

"Peppa, George, wake up! It's morning,"
says Mummy Pig brightly.

"Did the Tooth Fairy come?"
Daddy Pig asks.
"No," says Peppa sadly.

"Let's look under your pillow,"
says Daddy Pig.

"Look, Peppa! The Tooth Fairy
has been and she's left you a coin!"

Hee!
Hee!
Hee!

"Hooray! Hee! Hee! Hee!" Peppa laughs. "Grunt! Next time I will stay awake and I will see the Tooth Fairy! Hee! Hee!"